All About Me

What I Wear

By Meg Gaertner

level 1 little blue readers

www.littlebluehousebooks.com

Little Blue House is distributed by North Star Editions:
sales@northstareditions.com | 888-417-0195

Produced for Little Blue House by Red Line Editorial.

Photographs ©: Avava/iStockphoto, cover; shapecharge/iStockphoto, 4; kali9/iStockphoto, 7; FatCamera/iStockphoto, 8–9; monkeybusinessimages/iStockphoto, 11; wundervisuals/iStockphoto, 12–13; LightFieldStudios/iStockphoto, 15; VladTeodor/iStockphoto, 16 (top left); paci77/iStockphoto, 16 (top right); Milkos/iStockphoto, 16 (bottom left); Taek-sang Jeong/iStockphoto, 16 (bottom right)

Library of Congress Control Number: 2019908252

ISBN
978-1-64619-007-2 (hardcover)
978-1-64619-046-1 (paperback)
978-1-64619-085-0 (ebook pdf)
978-1-64619-124-6 (hosted ebook)

Printed in the United States of America
Mankato, MN
012020

About the Author

Meg Gaertner enjoys reading, writing, dancing, and being outside. She lives in Minnesota.

Table of Contents

shoe

What I Wear

I wear shoes.

I wear a shirt.

shirt

I wear shorts.

shorts

I wear pants.

pants

I wear a dress.

dress

I wear a jacket.

jacket

Glossary

dress

shirt

pants

shorts

Index